Author: Tracy Johns

Illustrations & Book Cover Design: J & I Publishing LLC

Editor: J & I Publishing LLC

Text and Illustrations Copyright © 2020 by Tracy Johns.

Address all inquiries to:

Email: littlebremar@gmail.com

      melanatedvoicesllc@gmail.com

ISBN-13: 978-1-7359019-0-9

Little Bremar
"I am Somebody"

Written by

Tracy Johns

Dedication

Dedicated to
My Three Sons
Mark, Brandon and Brennan
Who you are is what I am.
With all my love, I thank you
for being my inspiration
and energy especially for
this part of my journey.

"Ok, scholars, does everyone have their book bags?"

"Yesssssssss," most of the students answer.

"And I have my speech in my folder, Miss Brown!" Myla yells out.

"Me too," the other students join in excitedly.

But in the middle of the line,
Bremar stands with his head
down. Miss Brown walks over
and asks, "Do you have your speech?"

"Yes, ma'am."
"But do I have to say it tomorrow?"

Pushing her way through,
Myla says: "What are
you so scared of?
It's just family day."

Just family day!

This is the big day!

The day when all families come to our classroom.

"How was school, son?"
"Today, I quit!"
"Wait, what?" His mother
looks surprised.

"Yes, I quit. I am not going
back. Tomorrow is the big
day and I am scared because
so many people will be staring
at me.

What if
everyone laughs?

What if I...
What if I ...
forget my words?"

"Ok, ok, slow down. Did we practice?"

"Yes."

"Do you know it?"

"Yes."

"Then why do you think you will forget it?"

"Mom, I am the very last one!"

Listening closely, Bremar's mother whispers:

"Son, just because you are last does not mean you will forget."

"The words are in you.

Sweet dreams.

Good night!"

"Good morning, scholars. Everyone looks so fancy."

"I have my tutu on," Myla says, twirling.

The families have arrived, and one by one the students begin their speeches.

Finally, Miss Brown calls out: "Bremar Johns!"

Slowly he walks to the microphone, looks at Myla.....

who gives him a huge smile, and he begins.

"I am somebody
and I am
important
to the world.

I can dream to be
whatever it is
I think I can
become.

Today, I will work
my best, to become
smarter than I
was yesterday.
Don't you know?

I am somebody!"

Bremar winks at his mom
and walks past his classmates
with his head held high
giving out fist pumps!

His mother was right.
The words were in him, and
they came out just when he
needed them.

To all the little scholars around
the world, always remember
who you are.

I am Somebody and
I am important to this world.
I can dream to be
Whatever it is I think I can become.

Today, I will work my best,
To become smarter than
I was yesterday.
Don't you know?

I am Somebody!

Scan Code to watch the Read Aloud

Author Biography

Tracy Johns has been an educator and community organizer for many years. She works tirelessly to help children see themselves in the characters she creates. Her debut children's book is a part of one in a series of *"Little Bremar"* books.

Years ago, she created the affirmation "I am Somebody" which was a **Call to Action** to ensure that her students were aware of their unlimited potential. Today, the Call to Action has been expanded to include melanated characters in story books to enable children of color the opportunity to embrace their beauty in literature.

In 2020, she was awarded by the Pittsburgh Pirates and PNC with a Teacher Appreciation Award. However, her greatest recognition comes from being the mother of her sons Mark, Brandon and Brennan.

Made in the USA
Middletown, DE
04 December 2020